The Petal Fairies

For Danielle Dawkins,
who has lots of magic of her own!

Special thanks to
Narinder Dhami

ORCHARD BOOKS
338 Euston Road, London NW1 3BH
Orchard Books Australia
Level 17/207 Kent Street, Sydney, NSW 2000
A Paperback Original

First published in 2007 by Orchard Books

© 2008 Rainbow Magic Limited.
A HIT Entertainment company. Rainbow Magic
is a trademark of Rainbow Magic Limited.
Reg. U.S. Pat. & Tm. Off. And other countries.

HiT entertainment

Cover illustrations © Georgie Ripper 2007
Inside illustrations © Orchard Books 2007

A CIP catalogue record for this book is available
from the British Library.

ISBN 978 1 84616 462 0

1 3 5 7 9 10 8 6 4 2

Printed and bound in China

Orchard Books is a division of Hachette Children's Books

www.orchardbooks.co.uk

Danielle
the Daisy
Fairy

by Daisy Meadows

ORCHARD BOOKS

www.rainbowmagic.co.uk

Jack Frost's
Ice Castle

Blossom Lake

Picnic Spot

The Park

Petal Perfection
Flower Shop

Blossom Village
High St

Rainbow Falls Gardens

Chaney Court Flower Show

I need the magic petals' powers,
To give my castle garden flowers.
And so I use my magic well
To work against the fairies' spell.

From my wand ice magic flies,
Frosty bolt through fairy skies.
And this crafty spell I weave
To bring the petals back to me.

Contents

A Mysterious Message

"Oh!" Rachel Walker panted as she trudged up the steep hill. "I'm really out of breath, Kirsty."

"Me, too," Kirsty Tate, Rachel's best friend, agreed. "Even Buttons looks a bit tired, and you know how he usually bounces around."

Buttons, the Walkers' shaggy dog,

was trotting along on his lead beside Rachel, his pink tongue hanging out.

"It'll be worth it when we get to the top, girls," called Rachel's dad. He was walking behind them with Mrs Walker and Kirsty's parents, carrying the picnic basket. "The view will be fantastic."

A few moments later, Rachel and Kirsty reached the top of the hill.

Both girls gasped with delight as
they gazed around.
"You were right, Dad,"
Rachel smiled.
"It was worth it,"
Kirsty added.
The sun was
shining and the
countryside that
was spread out
below them
looked beautiful.
Lush green fields
stretched away in
every direction and,
nestled in a little
valley, the girls could see
the thatched cottages of
Blossom Village.

"Blossom Village almost looks Fairyland-size from here!" Rachel whispered to Kirsty.

Kirsty laughed. She and Rachel knew more about fairies than anyone else in the world! The fairies were their special friends, and the girls had visited Fairyland many times.

"Look, there's Blossom Hall," remarked Mr Tate, pointing at a bigger building beyond the village. The Tates and the Walkers were spending their Easter holidays in the old Tudor house that was now a country hotel.

"Even that looks small from up here!"

Kirsty and Rachel
shared a smile as they
gazed at Blossom
Hall. Their stay at
the old hotel had
led to a whole new
fairy adventure. On
their first day at the
hall, they had met Tia

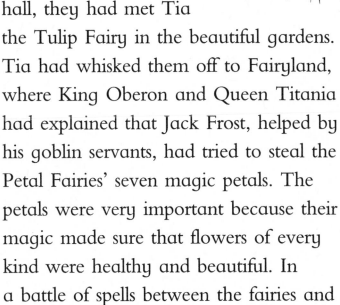

the Tulip Fairy in the beautiful gardens.
Tia had whisked them off to Fairyland,
where King Oberon and Queen Titania
had explained that Jack Frost, helped by
his goblin servants, had tried to steal the
Petal Fairies' seven magic petals. The
petals were very important because their
magic made sure that flowers of every
kind were healthy and beautiful. In
a battle of spells between the fairies and

Jack Frost, the petals had spun away and become lost in the human world. Jack Frost had sent his goblins to get them back, and now Rachel and Kirsty were hoping to help the fairies find the magic petals before the goblins did.

"Where shall we have our picnic?" asked Mrs Tate. She glanced up at the sky, where a big bank of cloud was threatening to cover the sun. "Oh dear, I do hope it isn't going to rain. The weather forecast said it might."

"Well, I brought a big umbrella,

14

in case," Mr Walker replied, "but let's
hope it holds off until we get home."

"Look, there's a nice spot over there by
the stream," Kirsty said, pointing across
the top of the hill. "That might be
a good place for our picnic."

"Good idea," Mr Walker agreed.

The stream was narrow but
crystal-clear, the
water bubbling and
flowing over
rocks and
pebbles. The
girls could see
that it ran
down the other
side of the hill
towards a cluster
of trees.

"Look, Rachel," Kirsty said
in a low voice as their
parents unpacked the
picnic basket. "The
daisies all around us
are wilting!"

"I know," Rachel
whispered back.
"I noticed when we were
walking up the hill. I hope we find
Danielle the Daisy Fairy's magic
petal today!"

"Yes, we've found five petals already,
but we need all seven," Kirsty added.

Rachel nodded solemnly. Both girls
knew that they had to return all the
petals to Fairyland for Petal Magic to
work properly and keep flowers in the
human world blooming brightly.

"This is a lovely spot," said
Mrs Walker, as she poured water
into Buttons' bowl. "I hope that long
walk has given you all an appetite."

Rachel and Kirsty nodded
enthusiastically as Mr Tate opened the
picnic basket and began handing out
packets of sandwiches and crisps.
As they ate, Buttons munched on some
dog treats.

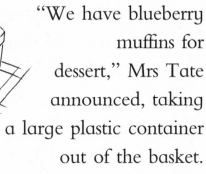

"We have blueberry muffins for dessert," Mrs Tate announced, taking a large plastic container out of the basket.

"Yum!" said Rachel happily.

"Just what I was going to say!" laughed her dad.

Kirsty and Rachel ate their sandwiches, enjoying the view. As Kirsty was finishing off her last sandwich, she gazed at the little stream bubbling its way down the hill towards the patch of trees. *I wonder where it ends up?* she thought.

Suddenly, to Kirsty's amazement, she saw a beautiful cloud of brilliant silver fairy dust rising from the trees.

Kirsty almost choked on the last bite of her sandwich! As she watched, the silvery sparkles began to drift through the air towards her.

Kirsty knew she and Rachel had to make sure their parents didn't spot the fairy dust. Quickly, she nudged Rachel

who was sitting next to her. Rachel
glanced up, and her eyes widened.

"Look, everyone!" Rachel said quickly,
pointing in the opposite direction.
"There's Leafley village with its field
of sunflowers."

Everyone except Kirsty turned to
·look where Rachel was pointing.

Meanwhile, Kirsty watched excitedly
as the silvery sparkles began to form
themselves into words, floating in
mid-air in front of her:

Look around, there's more to see,
A fairy friend says follow me!

Then the cloud of sparkles streamed
away and vanished on the breeze.

Still tingling with excitement, Kirsty turned to her mother. "Mum, is it OK if Rachel and I go exploring before we have our muffins?" she asked eagerly. Mrs Tate nodded. "Don't go far, though," said Mr Walker, "and be back in half an hour." Rachel and Kirsty scrambled to their feet and hurried off, following the stream towards the little wood.

"The sparkles spelled out a message, Rachel!" Kirsty told her friend, her eyes shining, and she repeated the little poem.

"One of the Petal Fairies must have sent it," Rachel guessed, her face alight with excitement.

The girls soon reached the trees. As they stood on the edge of the wood, wondering where to go next, they heard a soft whooshing sound. Suddenly, tiny silver sparkles began shooting out from behind a leafy oak tree.

The girls hurried over.

"Hi, girls," Danielle the Daisy Fairy called, peeping out from behind the tree trunk and grinning at them. "I've been waiting for you!"

Daisy, Daisy

Danielle danced out from behind the tree as Kirsty and Rachel glanced at each other in delight. The little fairy looked very daisy-like herself in a bright yellow top and a white skirt edged with pink. Her wings were pink-tipped too, and a daisy-shaped clip held back her long blonde hair.

"It's great to see you, girls," Danielle
declared. "And I really need your help.
One of Jack Frost's goblins has found
my magic Daisy Petal, and until I get
it back, daisies and all the white flowers
in the world will be dying!"

"Oh!" Rachel gasped.
"Is the goblin in
this wood?"
Danielle nodded.
"Follow me,"
she cried. "But
remember, girls, the
goblins have a wand
of Jack Frost's icy magic
to help them. So we must be careful!"
Danielle flew off, and Kirsty and
Rachel followed the tiny, sparkling
figure deeper into the woods. After

a few moments Danielle came to a stop behind a large oak tree with a thick gnarled trunk. She beckoned to the girls, putting her finger to her lips.

   Kirsty and Rachel peered around the tree trunk. In front of them was a large clearing, the green grass studded with wilting daisies. A goblin sat on a rock in the middle of the clearing, making

a daisy chain. He had collected a big pile of the flowers, ready to add to the chain, and they lay in a heap next to him.

"Look at the daisies the goblin has collected," Danielle whispered.

Rachel and Kirsty stared at the heap of daisies and immediately noticed that they looked fresh and healthy, with their bright yellow centres and petals edged with pink. The girls knew that that meant the magic petal must be very close by.

The goblin's chain was growing quickly, and he was singing a silly made-up song as he threaded the daisies together.

"Daisy, daisy, I'm not lazy," he sang loudly, twirling a daisy in his knobbly

green hand. *"Daisy, daisy, I'm not crazy! I just love my daisies!"*

Kirsty clapped her hands over her ears. "He's all out of tune!" she complained.

"The other goblins can't be far away," Rachel said in a low voice. "Jack Frost told them to stick together this time, remember?"

"This one doesn't have the wand, either," Danielle pointed out. "Let's try and get my petal back before the others turn up."

But before they could do anything, they heard noises from the other side of the wood.

A few moments later a large group of noisy goblins burst into the clearing. Rachel, Kirsty and Danielle glanced at each other in dismay, especially when they saw the icy wand, which was held by the smallest goblin.

"What are you doing?" demanded a big goblin, going over to the one with the daisies.

"Making a daisy chain," the seated goblin replied.

"Lazybones!" snapped the smallest goblin. "We've been searching all over the hill for the magic petal, and you've been sitting here having a nice rest!"

"It's not fair!" the big goblin grumbled. "I'm telling Jack Frost!" Looking annoyed, the seated goblin threw down his daisy chain and jumped off the rock. "All right!" he snapped.

"I'll help you look now." And he
tramped sulkily off across the clearing,
poking amongst the patches of daisies.

Rachel, Kirsty and Danielle watched
as all the others followed, except for the

big goblin. With
a naughty grin on
his face, he picked
up the long daisy
chain and draped
it around his
shoulders like
a feather boa.

"Hey!" The goblin who
had made the chain suddenly noticed,
and dashed over to him. "Give that
back!" he screeched. "It's mine!"

"Shan't!" the big goblin retorted.
"I look lovely."

Furious, the first goblin grabbed one end of the daisy chain. But before he could pull it away, the big goblin grabbed the other end of it and the delicate chain immediately broke and fell apart.

"Now look what you've done!" yelled the first goblin as they both threw the broken ends down on the ground.

"It was your fault!" the big goblin grumbled sulkily. He drew back his large, knobbly foot and kicked the neat pile of daisies into the air, sending them all flying.

❀ 33 ❀

"You lot go and search this wood for the magic petal!" he roared at the others when he saw them watching him. "We must find it before those pesky fairies do!"

All the goblins stomped off across the clearing, searching for the petal, and the big goblin came straight towards the tree where Danielle and the girls were hiding.

As the goblin came closer, Rachel noticed something magical. Everywhere the goblin stepped, the daisies around his feet bloomed brightly!

But as soon as he moved away from them, they died again.

Rachel knew this could only mean one thing.

"Look at the goblin's foot when he lifts it up," she whispered to Kirsty and Danielle. "I'm sure that the magic petal is stuck underneath!"

Step By Step

Danielle and the girls watched closely as the goblin lifted his foot to take another step. Sure enough, the sparkling, white magic petal was stuck to the underside of his big green heel.

"How are we going to get it away from him?" asked Rachel anxiously.

Kirsty thought hard for a moment.

"I think I have an idea…" she said
thoughtfully. "Danielle, could you turn
us into fairies, please?"

"Of course!" Danielle replied.

She flew above Rachel and Kirsty
and, with a flick of her fairy wand,
showered them with glittering magical
sparkles. The girls felt the familiar rush
of excitement as they began to shrink.
Within seconds they were the same size
as Danielle, and had shining fairy
wings on their backs.

"Let's go!" Kirsty declared, flying off into the clearing. Rachel and Danielle followed.

The other goblins had disappeared into the wood now, so that only the big goblin was still searching the clearing. He seemed very annoyed as he looked half-heartedly for the magic petal. Kirsty wondered what he'd do if he knew it was stuck to his very own foot.

"Hello!" she called, hovering above him with Rachel and Danielle beside her.

The goblin glanced up. "Pesky fairies!" he muttered sulkily. "Always turning up out of the blue."

"You've been working very hard, haven't you?" said Kirsty kindly.

The goblin frowned. "Yes, I have!" he snapped.

"So you must be tired," Kirsty went on. "After all, that other goblin had a good rest, but you didn't."

"Yes, it wasn't fair!" the big goblin moaned. Rachel and Danielle grinned at each other as they realised what Kirsty was planning!

"Well, now it's your turn to have a rest," Rachel chimed in. "Why don't you lie down?" And she pointed at the rock where the first goblin had been sitting.

The goblin yawned. "Maybe I will."

As the goblin walked back to the rock, the daisies at his feet again bloomed and wilted as he passed.

Danielle, Kirsty and Rachel glanced
anxiously at each other, but luckily the
goblin didn't notice. He sat down on
the rock and yawned again.

Winking at the girls, Danielle lifted
her wand, and a shower of sparkles
floated down onto the broken daisy
chain. The daisies immediately
bunched themselves
up into a soft,
snuggly white
pillow.
The goblin looked
at the comfy pillow.
"Nobody will notice if I take a quick
snooze," he said to himself, glancing
quickly around the clearing to
make sure the other goblins were
nowhere in sight. "After all, I have

worked the hardest today…"

And he put his head on the daisy pillow, lifted his feet onto the rock and closed his eyes. Now Danielle, Kirsty and Rachel could see the magic petal sparkling at them from the bottom of the goblin's foot.

They waited, hardly daring to move, until they heard heavy, rumbling snores echoing through the clearing.

"The goblin's asleep," Kirsty whispered. "Now we can peel the petal off his foot. Come on!"

Quickly all three of them flew down to the snoring goblin. They were just peeling the petal carefully away from his toes when they heard a noise behind them. A second later the other goblins came crashing through the trees into the clearing. The three friends gasped in dismay.

"Hey!" the smallest goblin shouted angrily, pointing at the goblin on the rock. "He's having a rest while we're doing all the work!"

"Look!" yelled another. "Fairies! I bet they're looking for the magic petal. Let's get them!"

And all the goblins rushed across the clearing, straight towards Danielle, Kirsty and Rachel.

Danielle in Trouble

At that moment, the goblin on the rock woke up and saw Danielle and the girls.

"Help!" he yelled, lashing out at them. "I'm being attacked by fairies!"

Danielle, Rachel and Kirsty had no choice but to leave the petal behind and fly quickly up into the air to

escape from the goblin on the rock, as
well as the others who were charging
towards them.

"What do we do now?"
asked Kirsty, as they
hovered above the
rock, looking
down at the petal
which was now
hanging off the
goblin's foot.

"I'll get rid of these pesky
fairies!" boasted the smallest goblin
eagerly, lifting Jack Frost's wand.

"*I don't want a doggie, a pig or
a whale,*" he shouted. "*But send to
that rock big pieces of hail!*" And
the smallest goblin pointed the wand
at the rock.

"Don't point that thing at me!"
shouted the big goblin in alarm,
jumping up and running for cover. As
he did so, the magic petal fell off his
foot and landed on the rock.

Danielle immediately swooped down
to grab it, closely followed by Kirsty
and Rachel. But, suddenly, big, icy
pieces of hail began to rain down onto
the rock from the sky.

Kirsty gasped in horror when she saw how huge the hailstones were. *It's like being pelted with enormous frozen footballs!* she thought, as she and her friends dodged this way and that to avoid being hit.

Just as Danielle reached out towards the Daisy Petal, a piece of hailstone struck her shoulder and sent her spinning towards the ground. Rachel and Kirsty immediately whizzed to her aid, managing to catch her in mid air.

They each took one of the
fairy's arms and helped her
fly safely to the edge of
the clearing, away
from the
hail storm.
"Are you
OK, Danielle?"
Kirsty asked
anxiously as
Rachel looked
at the tiny fairy
with a worried
frown. Danielle
was looking
very shaken.
"I'm OK, but I've
lost my wand!" Danielle
exclaimed, rubbing her shoulder.

"I must have dropped it when
I was hit."

"Look, there it is!" Rachel said,
pointing back at the rock. Through the
shower of hailstones they could see the
wand lying next to the magic petal.

Danielle, Kirsty and Rachel looked at
each other, wondering what to do.

Just then, there was a shout from one of the goblins.

"There's the magic petal!" he cried, pointing at the rock where the petal sparkled among the hailstones.

"And that's a fairy wand next to it!" added another in glee.

The goblins gathered around the rock,
just out of reach of the hailstones,
staring at the petal and Danielle's wand.

"The fairies can't get the magic petal
now, but neither can we!" the big
goblin said, scowling at the goblin with
the wand. "What a stupid spell!"

"Danielle, perhaps if Rachel and
I were human again, we could
dodge the hailstones and
grab the petal,"
Kirsty suggested.

Danielle's wings
drooped. "But
I can't turn you
back to normal
without my
wand," she
said glumly.

"Maybe I can help!" said a kind voice behind them.

Danielle, Kirsty and Rachel spun round. To their amazement, a girl was standing among the trees, smiling at them!

A Helping Hand

Kirsty and Rachel were so surprised, neither of them could say a word. The fairies were meant to be a secret! The two girls were the only humans who knew about them. What was going to happen now?

"Don't worry," the girl said quickly, "I won't tell anyone. I've always wanted to see a fairy, but I never, ever thought I would!"

Danielle smiled and turned to Rachel and Kirsty. "It's OK," she said. "She's going to be our friend!" And she fluttered over to the girl. "I'm Danielle, this is Rachel and this is Kirsty."

"My name's Rebecca Wilson," the girl replied, watching with delight as Danielle, Rachel and Kirsty hovered in front of her.

"Well, Rebecca, we really need your help!" Danielle explained. "But you must promise never to tell anyone that you've met the fairies."

"I promise," Rebecca said solemnly.

Quickly Danielle explained about Jack Frost and his goblins stealing the magic petals.

Rebecca looked horrified. "Jack Frost must be very mean!" she said. "What can I do to help?"

"Oh!" Kirsty gasped, as she suddenly thought of something. "Rachel, what a shame we didn't bring one of our umbrellas with us!"

"Yes, we could have given it to
Rebecca and she could have got
through the hailstones and grabbed the
petal for us," Rachel agreed.

Rebecca was
looking puzzled.
"I've got an
umbrella in my
backpack," she
said, reaching in
her bag and
taking out a pink
umbrella. "But
I can't see any hailstones!"
Danielle laughed. "Come and look!"
Danielle and the girls led Rebecca
to the edge of the clearing where the
goblins were still standing around
the rock.

"I'll get the magic petal!" one of them was boasting. He reached out for it and then jumped back quickly as hailstones pelted his hand. "Ouch!"

"Leave this to me," said another goblin importantly. He made a grab for the petal and then he, too, squealed in dismay. "Ow, that hurt!"

"Jack Frost wants that petal!" the big goblin said urgently. "And if we take him that fairy's wand as well, he'll be really pleased with us!"

"Now I see why you need the umbrella!" whispered Rebecca. "I'll hold it for you."

"Thank you!" chorused Danielle, Rachel and Kirsty.

Rebecca walked bravely out into the clearing with Danielle and the girls flying beside her.

"Er – *Hail, Hail, please go away nice and quick,*" the smallest goblin chanted, trying desperately to think of a spell to get rid of the hail.

"That's rubbish!" the others jeered. Suddenly the goblins noticed Rebecca and the girls. Quickly Rebecca opened her umbrella and pointed it straight at the goblins. They shrieked with fright and backed away a little. Rebecca hurried forward and held the umbrella over the rock so that the hailstones bounced off it harmlessly.

"They're going to get the magic petal *and* the fairy wand!" shouted the big goblin, as Danielle, Rachel and Kirsty darted forward under cover of the umbrella. "We need that spell!"

"We don't like this nasty hail!" the smallest goblin yelled. *"I wish we could all go home!"*

"That doesn't even rhyme!" another goblin yelled furiously.

Meanwhile, Danielle had grabbed her wand and Kirsty and Rachel had picked up the magic petal between them.

"Hail, hail, go away," shouted the smallest goblin, waving the wand, *"And don't come back until May!"*

64

Immediately the hailstones stopped.
Danielle, Rachel, Kirsty and Rebecca
exchanged a panicked look as all
the goblins hurried forwards to block
their way.

"Leave my friends alone!" Rebecca
said bravely, waving her umbrella.

"Shan't!" scoffed the smallest goblin
as the others stuck their tongues out
rudely. "We're taking that petal to
Jack Frost!"

Daisy Delight

Rachel thought fast. She turned to
Danielle and whispered something in
her ear.

Danielle's worried face broke into
a big smile. She waved her wand
back and forth, and a shower of
fairy dust fell onto the daisy pillow,
still lying on the ground. Quickly the

magic sparkles transformed the pillow
back into a daisy chain.

As Danielle, the girls and Rebecca
watched, the daisy chain flew up into
the air and began to wind itself tightly
around the goblins.

"Help!" shrieked the smallest goblin.
"What's happening?" He raised his
wand to try to cast another spell, but
he was held fast by the chain of daisies.

"Let us go!" yelled the biggest goblin furiously as the daisy chain tied itself into a neat little bow.

"It's a parcel of goblins!" said Rachel with a grin, watching as the goblins struggled helplessly.

"My petal magic has made the daisy chain extra-strong!" laughed Danielle, as she, Kirsty, Rachel and Rebecca hurried out of the clearing. Behind

them they could hear the goblins fighting and arguing as they tried to break out of the daisy chain.

"It will take the goblins a while to get free," Danielle went on. "And, by then, I'll have taken my beautiful petal back to Fairyland!"

With a wave of Danielle's wand, the Daisy Petal that Kirsty and Rachel were holding shrank down to its Fairyland size and floated to Danielle. Another sprinkling of fairy magic made Rachel and Kirsty their normal size again too.

Rebecca looked
very surprised.
"I didn't know
you were girls too!"
she exclaimed.

The girls nodded.

"Rachel and Kirsty
are best friends of the
fairies," Danielle explained. "And now
you're one of our friends too!"

"I'm glad I was able to help!" said
Rebecca as Rachel and Kirsty grinned
at her. "Now I'd better get back or my
family will wonder where I've got to.
We're having a picnic on the other side
of the wood."

"Thank you for your help, and
goodbye!" Danielle called, waving.

"Yes, thank you, Rebecca!" said

Rachel and Kirsty together.

"Goodbye!" Rebecca called, as she set off through the trees. "I'll never, ever forget the day I met a real fairy!"

"We'd better go too, Rachel," said Kirsty when Rebecca had disappeared.

Danielle nodded. "Thank you so much for all your help, girls," she told them. "Now, you only have one more magic petal to find. Good luck!" And, clutching her Daisy Petal tightly, Danielle disappeared in a shower of fairy dust.

"Wasn't Rebecca nice?" remarked Rachel, as they hurried back to their parents.

Kirsty nodded. "I don't know what we'd have done if she hadn't come along!" she replied, as Buttons rushed to meet them, tail wagging.

Their parents were snoozing on the picnic blanket, but Mrs Tate sat up as the girls ran over.

"We've saved you some muffins," she said kindly, handing them out. "Did you have a nice walk?"

The girls nodded, laughing at Buttons who was now rolling around on his back in a patch of springy white daisies.

"Well, I didn't notice all those beautiful daisies when we were on our way up the hill!" Mrs Tate said, looking around her. All over the hill the grass was now starred with the little white flowers. "Aren't they pretty?"

Rachel and Kirsty nodded and shared a secret smile. All the daisies were blooming beautifully now that Danielle's magic petal was back in Fairyland where it belonged!

The Petal Fairies

Danielle the Daisy Fairy has got her magic petal back. Now Rachel and Kirsty must help

Ella the Rose Fairy

TIA THE TULIP FAIRY
978-1-84616-457-6

PIPPA THE POPPY FAIRY
978-1-84616-458-3

LOUISE THE LILY FAIRY
978-1-84616-459-0

CHARLOTTE THE
SUNFLOWER FAIRY
978-1-84616-460-6

OLIVIA THE ORCHID FAIRY
978-1-84616-461-3

DANIELLE THE DAISY FAIRY
978-1-84616-462-0

ELLA THE ROSE FAIRY
978-1-84616-464-4

Win Rainbow Magic goodies!

In every book in the Rainbow Magic Petal Fairies series (books 43-49) there is a hidden picture of a petal with a secret letter in it. Find all seven letters and re-arrange them to make a special Petal Fairies word, then send it to us. Each month we will put the entries into a draw and select one winner to receive a Rainbow Magic Sparkly T-shirt and Goody Bag!

Send your entry on a postcard to Rainbow Magic Fun Day Competition, Orchard Books, 338 Euston Road, London NW1 3BH. Australian readers should write to Hachette Children's Books, Level 17/207 Kent Street, Sydney, NSW 2000. New Zealand readers should write to Rainbow Magic Competition, 4 Whetu Place, Mairangi Bay, Auckland, NZ. Don't forget to include your name and address. Only one entry per child. Final draw: 30th April 2008.

Good luck!

Have you checked out the

website at:
www.rainbowmagic.co.uk

by Daisy Meadows

The Pet Keeper Fairies

Katie the Kitten Fairy	ISBN	978 1 84616 166 7
Bella the Bunny Fairy	ISBN	978 1 84616 170 4
Georgia the Guinea Pig Fairy	ISBN	978 1 84616 168 1
Lauren the Puppy Fairy	ISBN	978 1 84616 169 8
Harriet the Hamster Fairy	ISBN	978 1 84616 167 4
Molly the Goldfish Fairy	ISBN	978 1 84616 172 8
Penny the Pony Fairy	ISBN	978 1 84616 171 1

The Fun Day Fairies

Megan the Monday Fairy	ISBN	978 184616 188 9
Tallulah the Tuesday Fairy	ISBN	978 1 84616 189 6
Willow the Wednesday Fairy	ISBN	978 1 84616 190 2
Thea the Thursday Fairy	ISBN	978 1 84616 191 9
Freya the Friday Fairy	ISBN	978 1 84616 192 6
Sienna the Saturday Fairy	ISBN	978 1 84616 193 3
Sarah the Sunday Fairy	ISBN	978 1 84616 194 0

Holly the Christmas Fairy	ISBN	978 1 84362 661 9
Summer the Holiday Fairy	ISBN	978 1 84362 960 3
Stella the Star Fairy	ISBN	978 1 84362 869 9
Kylie the Carnival Fairy	ISBN	978 1 84616 175 9
Paige the Pantomime Fairy	ISBN	978 1 84616 047 9
The Rainbow Magic Treasury	ISBN	978 1 84616 209 1
Fairy Fashion Dress-up Book	ISBN	978 1 84616 371 5
Fairy Friends Sticker Book	ISBN	978 1 84616 370 8

Coming soon:

Flora the Fancy Dress Fairy	ISBN	978 1 84616 505 4

All priced at £3.99. *Holly the Christmas Fairy, Summer the Holiday Fairy,*
Stella the Star Fairy, Kylie the Carnival Fairy, Paige the Pantomime Fairy and
Flora the Fancy Dress Fairy are priced at £5.99. *The Rainbow Magic Treasury* is priced at £12.99.
Fairy Fashion Dress-up Book and *Fairy Friends Sticker Book* are priced at £3.99.
Rainbow Magic books are available from all good bookshops, or can be ordered
direct from the publisher: Orchard Books, PO BOX 29, Douglas IM99 1BQ
Credit card orders please telephone 01624 836000
or fax 01624 837033 or visit our Internet site: www.wattspub.co.uk
or e-mail: bookshop@enterprise.net for details.

To order please quote title, author and ISBN and your full name and address.
Cheques and postal orders should be made payable to 'Bookpost plc.'
Postage and packing is FREE within the UK (overseas customers should add £2.00 per book).
Prices and availability are subject to change.

Look out for the Dance Fairies!

TASHA
THE TAP DANCE FAIRY
978-1-84616-493-4

REBECCA
THE ROCK 'N' ROLL FAIRY
978-1-84616-492-7

BETHANY
THE BALLET FAIRY
978-1-84616-490-3

JADE
THE DISCO FAIRY
978-1-84616-491-0

IMOGEN
THE ICE DANCE FAIRY
978-1-84616-497-2

JESSICA
THE JAZZ FAIRY
978-1-84616-495-8

SASKIA
THE SALSA FAIRY
978-1-84616-496-5

Available Now!